Milly and Molly

For my grandchildren
Thomas, Harry, Ella and Madeleine

Milly, Molly and Pet Day

Copyright© Milly Molly Books, 2003

Gill Pittar and Cris Morrell assert the moral right to
be recognised as the author and illustrator of this work.

Published by
Milly Molly Books
P O Box 539
gisborne, New Zealand
email: books@millymolly.com

Printed by Rhythm Consolidated Berhad, Malaysia

ISBN: 1-86972-010-5

10   9   8   7   6   5   4   3   2   1

Milly, Molly
and
Pet Day

"We may look different
but we feel the same."

It was almost Pet Day again.
Milly and Molly were given a month to
groom Marmalade and Tom Cat,
and teach them to come when called.

2

Marmalade and Tom Cat loved to
be brushed as they lay in the sun.

They even put up with having their
whiskers combed.

Marmalade and Tom Cat came running
when called for dinner.

But if it wasn't for dinner, they wouldn't
come when called.

6

Molly's mother said, "Everyone at school
will be having the same problem. On the day,
Marmalade and Tom Cat will be perfect."

Milly's mother said, "It simply takes the three
P's - Practice, Persistence and Patience."

At last it was Pet Day. Marmalade and Tom
Cat were bundled into their travelling box.

Marmalade began to yowl and search the corners for a hole to get out.

Tom Cat cowered in the corner with his
ears flat and his tail all a twitch.

The school playing field looked like a zoo.

The loud speaker boomed ORDER!

14

"Please stand opposite your pet and call it."

The calling was frantic.

There was pandemonium.

The horse kicked his hoofs in the air.
The dogs chased the cats.
The guinea pigs hid in the long grass.
The goat ran straight for the rose garden.
The lamb latched onto the nearest big toe.
The piglets headed for home.
The tortoise went into his shell.
And there was no sign of the mouse.

When everything was quiet, the tortoise
came out of his shell.

There was still no sign of the mouse.

The tortoise inched closer to Poppy.
She quietly urged him on.
But there was still no sign of the mouse.

The tortoise was almost there.
Suddenly, from the box in the middle,
out came the mouse.

It made a dash for Harry's trouser leg.
It ran so fast that, if you hadn't been
watching carefully, you may only have
noticed a blur.

The mouse had pipped the tortoise
at the winning post!

That night, as Milly and Molly stroked
Marmalade and Tom Cat to a purr, they
reassured them of their loyalty. "You might
not always come when called, but we would
never ever swap you for a mouse."

24

Milly, Molly and Pet Day

The value implicitly expressed in this story is 'loyalty' - being faithful to one's friends, family and country.

Milly and Molly remain loyal to Marmalade and Tom Cat when they don't win the prize on Pet Day. Winning isn't everything!

"We may look different but we feel the same".

Milly Molly ®

B O O K S

Other picture books in the Milly, Molly series include:

- Milly, Molly and Jimmy's Seeds   ISBN 1-86972-007-5

- Milly, Molly and Taffy Bogle   ISBN 1-86972-008-3

- Milly, Molly and Oink   ISBN 1-86972-009-1

- Milly, Molly and the Tree Hut   ISBN 1-86972-013-X

- Milly, Molly and Betelgeuse   ISBN 1-86972-011-3